The Children of L

I sing of a time that is legend,
I speak of a race that is myth,
I know of a place of enchantment,
I have known the Children of Lir . . .

MICHAEL SCOTT

The Children of Lir
An Irish Legend

Illustrated by Jim Fitzpatrick

A Magnet Book

For Courtney and Kristofer and Edwin

First published in 1986 as a Magnet paperback
by Methuen Children's Books Ltd
11 New Fetter Lane, London EC4P 4EE
Text copyright © 1986 Michael Scott
Illustrations copyright © 1986 Jim Fitzpatrick
Printed in Great Britain

ISBN 0 416 55000 2

'This will be the last time I will tell this tale, and I must hurry, because my brothers are waiting for me and they say that we must soon be gone. So, if you are listening I shall begin, and I will tell you the tale of the Children of Lir.

'My name is Fionnuala . . .'

Chapter One

'*I was a girl,*' Fionnuala began, '*when the world was very young. It was different then; it seemed bigger and there was always magic in the air. Creatures and animals who are gone now lived then; dragons on huge wings floated in the skies, there were monsters in the sea, and silver-horned unicorns ran wild in the forest. There were witches and warlocks, magicians and sorcerers in the world and not all of them were bad. Indeed, everyone knew a little magic.*

'*Not all the people were human either; there were giants and dwarves, trolls, goblins, and sprites. My own family were not human folk. My father was called Lir, and he was the Lord of the Sea and ruler of the Tir faoi Thuinn, the Land beneath the waves. He was one of the ancient Tuatha De Danann, the People of the Goddess Danu, who had come from their four magical cities across the sea to this green land. My mother was the most beautiful woman in all the De Dannan tribe, and she was called Eva.*

'*I suppose I should begin my story on the day my two younger brothers were born. It was a bright summer's day and my brother Aedh and I were swimming . . .*'

The Sleeping Queen

The young girl and boy dived into the ice-cold water together and struck out strongly towards the other side of the small pool. They did not swim like human children, who splashed and crashed noisily across the surface of the water, but rather they folded their arms by their sides and used their feet to push them along just beneath the surface, moving like seals or otters. Their toes had a thin web of skin between them – like a fish's fins – and they also had a tiny set of gills set into the sides of their throats which allowed them to breathe under water. The sea was their second home, and they could breathe and move just as easily under water as they could on dry land.

When they reached the far side of the lake their heads broke the surface at the same time and they rose from the water up on to the grassy bank in one smooth leap. They stood in the shade of some weeping-willow trees and shook themselves dry, and Fionnuala ran her hands through her hair and allowed the gentle summer breeze to blow it dry.

It would have been hard for a stranger to tell brother and sister apart, for, in features, looks, height and colouring they resembled one another. They might have been taken for twins, although Fionnuala was a year older than her brother. But people who knew them well knew that Fionnuala's hair was slightly longer and thicker than her brother's, and it had a dark green tint to it.

'What are we going to do for the rest of the day?' Aedh asked, breathing in deep lungfuls of the clear, clean air.

'Well, we'll go back home and get some lunch first,' Fionnuala said, pulling a twig from her hair, 'and then we will see how Mother is . . .'

There was a sudden crashing in the woods behind them and they both leaped to the water's edge, ready to dive to safety beneath the icy waters. Although they were in the gardens of their father's Fort, wild beasts still managed to wander past the guards and graze in the rich pastures close to the palace. If wolves or wild boars were hungry, they could be terribly dangerous.

A tree shook and a bush trembled, and then a twig snapped and a huge figure in bronze and leather armour brushed aside the branches and stepped out into the glade. There was a longsword strapped to his side and he carried a long flat-headed spear. Fionnuala and Aedh relaxed: it was only Martan, their father's bodyguard. He was red-faced and out of breath, for the day was very warm and he had run down from the Fort in his heavy armour.

'Your . . . your father, the King, wishes . . . wishes you to return . . . to the Fort . . . immediately,' he gasped, leaning on his long spear while he caught his breath.

'What's wrong?' Fionnuala asked quickly.

Martan shook his head. 'I don't know; your father just told me to fetch you as quickly as possible.'

The two children thanked him and, dressing quickly in their green and gold tunics, they set off at a run for the White Fort. They slipped in and out of the bushes without disturbing a leaf, leaped across the many tiny

streamlets without breaking step and vaulted over a fallen tree without stumbling. However, as soon as they had left the wood behind and were back on the pathway that led up to the palace they had to slow down. The sun was now behind them and was shining on the polished white stones and golden roof of the White Fort. The light was so blinding that, instead of climbing the hill to the main gate, they took one of the side paths that led around behind the Fort so that they were out of the glare and could see without squinting. They began to run again, laughing and calling, racing each other.

They burst into the kitchen side-by-side, both shouting that they had won . . . and then they suddenly stopped. Mairid, the fat old cook, and Fodhla, one of their mother's maids, were sitting by the huge white-sanded table, crying together. But before they could ask any questions, the heavy wooden door at the far end of the room opened and Mechar, their father's most trusted servant and friend appeared. He stopped when he saw them and beckoned them forward with his finger.

He was a tall, powerfully-built man, with a broad, square face and thick bushy eyebrows that made him seem angry-looking. He had spent many years in their father's army, and more from habit than anything else, he was always shouting at the servants and guards. But he treated the children as if they were his own. Without saying a word, he took them both by the hand and led them through the corridors of the Fort which were strangely empty. At this time of day they were usually busy with servants bustling to and fro.

'What's wrong, Mechar?' Fionnuala asked quietly, suddenly frightened by the strange look on his face and the empty hallways. But he only shook his head and smiled sadly, and all he would say was, 'Wait.'

He turned a corner and led them down a long flight of steps, which led to another corridor. This was a part of the palace where they had never been. It was dark and dim and there was a strong smell of seaweed and salt air about it. The walls here were not white and polished and sparkling like those in the rest of the Fort; they were dark and stained and there was a green fungus growing in the cracks between the stones. There were huge cobwebs everywhere, and some of them were so thick that they looked like grey blankets. There were burning torches set into rusted holders high on the walls, but they did little to light the way and only added to the strange mixture of smells.

Mechar stopped before a huge wooden door, and tapped on it gently with his fingertips. He then said something in the old language of the Tuatha De Danann and the door slowly creaked all the way open. The room inside was in total darkness.

Mechar then squatted down on the floor beside the two children. 'You must go in by yourselves,' he said softly. 'I cannot follow you.'

'What's in there?' Aedh asked, peering into the darkness.

'Go in and see,' Mechar said.

'But it's dark,' Aedh almost whispered.

'Go inside,' Mechar said, and placed one of his huge hands on each of their backs and gently eased them in through the doorway.

Once they stepped into the room they became aware of a dim blue light and at the same time the door swung silently closed and clicked shut behind them. The blue light seemed to be seeping up through the floor and out of the walls and down from the ceiling. It was a soft, warm, gentle light – rather like the morning sky on a summer's day. Once they got over the surprise and shock, Fionnuala and Aedh looked around in amazement. They had almost expected the room to be dark and dusty like the corridor, but it was sparkling, bright and clean.

The room was round and the walls, floor and ceiling were coloured in different shades of blue. Pictures of sea creatures had been painted on the walls in perfect detail and in glowing colours, and where the walls joined the floor there were more pictures, but this time of sea plants with long waving fronds, multi-coloured flowers and brightly coloured crabs and lobsters. The ceiling had been painted in such a way that it looked like the surface of the water seen from underneath, and for a moment the children were fooled into thinking that they were actually under water, and they felt the air rush in through the sides of their throats as their gills opened.

A door suddenly opened in the wall just in front of them, and blue-green light streamed into the room. A tall figure stepped into the doorway, sending a dark shadow dancing across the floor and up the wall. Fionnuala and Aedh took a few steps back until the strange being ahead of them raised one of its arms and the light died down, and they recognized their father. They ran to him and he hugged them both close.

Lir was a huge man; he was both tall and broad and he was the biggest of the De Danann people. Fionnuala was said to look most like her father, although his face was harder and sharper than hers and the green tinge in his short hair and beard was very obvious. His skin was also a slight shade of green and the webbing between his

fingers and toes was thicker and more noticeable than his children's. He was dressed in a short, knee-length tunic of silver and emerald, and there were rings and bracelets of purest coral around his fingers and wrists.

'My children,' he said softly, and stooping down, picked them both up, holding them in the crook of either arm.

'What is this place?' Aedh asked, his eyes wide and round in astonishment.

Lir, the Lord of the Sea, smiled sadly. 'This is a room I had hoped you would never have to see. There is a room like this in every Fort of the De Danann people but luckily, it is a room our people do not often have to use.' He slowly looked around. 'This is the place where the people of our race go when they feel that they are near to their time for Sleeping.'

'What is Sleeping, Father?' Fionnuala asked, suddenly deciding she didn't like the beautiful blue room.

'The human people would call it death,' Lir said slowly.

'But, Father,' Aedh said in a whisper, 'we are the People of the Goddess, we cannot die, we are immortal.'

Lir nodded his great head and his grey-green eyes clouded with tears. 'Although we may be immortal, little Aedh, we still need to rest. And that rest can last for up to a thousand years or more! I suppose you might say it is a sort of death.'

Lir's words made the young girl shiver. She looked at her father's face, and saw the pain and sadness in his eyes. 'Father,' she asked, her voice trembling, 'is it Mother?'

The King nodded and he knelt on the floor and put the children back on their feet. He then stood up and taking them both by the hand, led them into the second room.

It was smaller than the first, but painted in the same shades of blue, and the same blue light still shone from the stones. There was only one piece of furniture in this room – a long low bed made of a cream-coloured stone, decorated with polished and glowing sea-shells.

Eva, the Queen, their mother, lay on the bed.

She was dressed in her finest robes, and wore all her most precious jewellery – from the pale gold crown on her head, with its many precious jewels, to the golden sandals on her feet. Her eyes were closed and her hands were folded together across her stomach. She looked as if she were resting.

'She is Sleeping,' Lir said in a whisper, 'and here she will stay until she wakes. But she will be watching over you in her dreams; she told me so before she slept. And when you are in the hour of your greatest danger she will come to you.'

'When will Mother wake?' Aedh asked in a very small voice. 'I want her to wake up.'

'So do I,' Lir said softly. 'I don't know when she will wake, but it will be a long time, I think.' He looked down at the two children. 'Kiss her now for the last time, because you won't be able to come back to this room again.'

Fionnuala took Aedh's hand and together they walked to the side of their mother's stone bed and gently kissed her cheek. They walked over to their father and then they looked back; it was hard to believe that they wouldn't see her again for a long, long time. She looked as if she might wake up at any moment. They went into the other room and Lir closed the door. It glowed with a bright blue-white light and then faded into the wall and became part of it. The King looked down at his children.

'Before your mother came down to this room, she gave birth to twins, two boys. Your mother and I decided that we would call them Fiachra and Conn.' Lir leaned down and kissed his two children on the forehead. 'Mechar is outside, he will take you to your brothers. Fionnuala,' he added gently, 'you must be a mother to them both, and Aedh, you must be their guard and teacher.'

Chapter Two

'The years seemed to pass very quickly. The twins grew up into two wild little boys, and they were always up to mischief. Aedh and I often found them climbing the walls of the Fort or eating the unripened apples off the trees in the orchard and they often went swimming in the rushing rivers and deep lakes, where even a fully grown man might have been swept away or drowned. We had our hands full with them.

'Our father changed when our mother left us. He was not the smiling, laughing man he had once been, and his eyes would often cloud and become distant, when something – like a wild flower, or a snatch of our mother's favourite song – would remind him of her. He took little or no interest in the White Fort and spent most of his time in his Kingdom Beneath the Waves. Aedh and I did the best we could to keep the palace looking well, but it was a huge rambling place and it soon began to look run-down and neglected. A lot of the servants left when our father went away, and the few that remained couldn't do all the jobs that needed doing, and the white walls went unpolished and the golden roof soon lost its glitter and was streaked with dirt and bird droppings.

'We spent a lot of time at our grandfather's Fort on the banks of Lough Derg and the River Shannon. He was our mother's father, and was called Bov Dearg or Red Bov, because of his bright red hair and beard. At that time he was king of all Banba, as Ireland was called in those days.

'We usually spent our summers with him, and the year that I

A Little Magic

was sixteen, Aedh fifteen and Fiachra and Conn six years old was no different. That summer seemed to pass very quickly, and the leaves on the trees soon began to turn brown and golden. We knew Mechar would be coming for us shortly.

'But it was our father who came, not Mechar. He arrived on the very last day of summer, and I remember the day clearly, because that was the day he met Aife, our mother's sister ...'

Aife was beautiful. Even amongst the women of the Tuatha De Danann, who were the most beautiful women in all the world, she was regarded as one of the most beautiful of them all.

She was very tall – almost as tall as Lir – and she had a heart-shaped face that came to a point at her chin. The tips of her ears too were slightly pointed, and her bright green eyes slanted upwards a little. But her loveliest feature was her hair, which was coal-black and flowed down to her knees in a long shimmering cloak. What was even more unusual were the two thick bands of bright red hair that started just over her ears and ran through her own dark hair like fire.

She was standing by the gate with Bov, her father, when Lir rode through, and she met him again at the great feast that was held in his honour that night. They talked together and seemed to get on very well, and so, instead of riding back to the White Fort the following morning, Lir decided to stay at Bov's Fort for a few more weeks. He spent most of that time with Aife, and they went hunting and fishing together in the huge forests that surrounded the palace and the many rivers that ran close by.

They often took the four children for picnics on the banks of the river Shannon. The river was huge and seemed to flow on for ever. Once, when they were resting in the shade of a willow tree after eating a huge lunch, Aedh asked his father about the river.

Lir had smiled sadly. 'You might say a greedy girl made this river,' he said.

'How?' Aedh asked.

'Yes, tell us, Father,' Fiachra and Conn said together.

'Please,' Fionnuala added.

Lir smiled again and leaned back against the cool green grass. A shaft of sunlight fell on his face, and suddenly his hair and beard and even the colour of his skin looked exactly the same colour as the grass. The four children settled around him, the twins sitting side by side, chewing apples, Aedh, with his feet in the water and Fionnuala lying flat on her stomach with her chin cupped in her hands. Aife sat beneath the willow tree, carefully weaving long strands of grass together as she, too, listened to the story.

'Many years ago,' Lir began, 'when we were fighting the terrible Fir Bolg for this land, we decided that we should gather together all our knowledge and put it in one secret place, so that if we lost, our power and secrets would not be lost also.

'So, the most powerful sorcerers and magicians

transformed everything that we knew into seven hazel trees. Once a year these trees would bear fruit and whoever would be lucky enough to eat the fruit would have whatever knowledge it contained. But to protect the trees, the magicians grew them around a magical crystal well. It looked like an ordinary well, but a terrible water demon was trapped inside.

'Well, the trees were planted and the water demon set to guard them, and then the magicians went away. But they had scarcely left the forest when a small figure crept out of the bushes and walked over to the first tree.

'She was a young girl – not much older than you, Fionnuala – and she had seen everything. She was also very greedy, and she thought that if she ate the fruit of the Trees of Knowledge, she would be the most powerful woman in the world. So she reached up her hand to pluck the first fruit.

'And the demon woke.'

'It shot up out of the well in a huge fountain of water, and caught up the girl in its watery paws, carrying her high, high into the air. The water kept on coming and coming and coming, until it towered in the heavens almost touching the clouds. And then it fell. It cut a huge gash through the rich green land, flowing south and west, until it finally reached the broad Western Ocean.' Lir sat up suddenly. 'That is how the river was made . . . and the young girl's name was Sinann, which over the years became Shannon and that is how the river got its name.'

The four children looked at the river and thought of the greedy girl, Sinann. Their father stood up, and brushed grass off his sleeves. 'Come on,' he said, 'we'd better be heading back.'

Sometimes Lir and Aife would borrow one of Bov's boats and row out across Lough Derg with the children and watch the setting sun turn the waters the colour of bright shimmering gold.

Once, when they were out boating on the lake, a sudden storm blew up and they were forced to take shelter on one of the tiny islands that were scattered across the water. The storm didn't bother Lir or the children, but Aife didn't like rough waves – they made her sick. There was nothing to do on the island and the children soon got bored and wanted to go home, so, to pass the time, Aife showed them some of her magic.

First, she had Conn bring her a handful of sand from the beach and then she asked him what he would like her to turn it into.

'Can you turn it into gold?' Conn asked.

Aife smiled and covered Conn's tiny hand with her own small fingers. She closed her eyes and her lips moved in the strange musical language of the ancient Tuatha De Danann, a language that was even now beginning to die out and which the children barely knew. Immediately a bright green glow spread from her fingertips, and Conn began to giggle because it tickled. Aife stopped her low murmuring and the green glow died away. She spoke one more word and a bright red-gold light flashed out from between the boy's fingers, and then she told him he could open his hand. When he did, he found he was holding a lump of bright gold.

Aife turned to Fiachra. 'What would you like me to do?'

The little boy bent down and picked up a large pebble. 'Could you make this into a diamond?' he asked slowly and carefully, because he sometimes stuttered if he got excited or spoke too fast.

Aife took the pebble and cupped her hands around it. She then bent her head and breathed on the stone and Fionnuala and her father leaned forward to watch what was happening. They saw the stone begin to change colour, the rough greyness slowly disappearing to be replaced with a pale milky colour, which in turn changed to a crystal clearness. Aife smiled and held up the large, pure diamond between her finger and thumb, where it sparkled and glittered with hundreds of tiny rainbow colours.

She looked at Aedh, but he was ready and handed her a stick and asked her to turn it into a sword for him. Aife took the branch and pressed it down into the soft sand until it was completely buried. With her long pointed nails she traced out a strange curling pattern into the sand, and then she said something in the old speech. Immediately all the grains of sand began to shift and move, and the children watched in fascination as the shifting patterns almost spelt words they understood. Faster and faster the grains of sand moved, until they were nothing more than a blur – and then they stopped, and fell in a small pile over the spot where the stick was. Aife brushed away the sand and then pulled the end of the stick from the ground with her small, neat hands . . . only it wasn't a stick any more, it was a short, gleaming metal sword with a silver blade and a golden hilt.

She handed it over to Aedh and then turned to Fionnuala. 'And what would you have me do?' she asked gently.

The young girl smiled and then carefully parted the branches of a bush by her side and, very gingerly, handed over a tiny fuzzy caterpillar. 'Can you change this into a butterfly?'

Her aunt took the tiny wriggling creature on to her finger, blew on it once and then tossed it up into the air. Lir and the children clearly saw a silky cocoon appear around the creature, which almost immediately hardened into a wrinkled brown shell, which then cracked and a bright black and yellow butterfly appeared. It fluttered once or twice, testing its wings and then it drifted down and rested on Fionnuala's outstretched arm, its tissue-like wings still damp and beating gently.

'How can you do that?' Fionnuala asked in a whisper.

'My power is that of transformation, of changing,' Aife explained. 'I can change things, small things usually, but if I had my magic cloak for example, I could change that lake into milk or turn the distant mountains into glass.'

Fionnuala shivered. 'That's a frightening power,' she said. The butterfly beat its wings one last time to dry them and then fluttered off, twisting and darting through the trees.

Aife shrugged. 'Oh, mine is only a small talent; my father is a far stronger magician and sorcerer than I will ever be.'

Lir stood up, rubbing his hands against his back which had gone stiff from sitting in the one position for so long. 'Look, the storm is dying down,' he said. 'We might as well head back to your grandfather's Fort.'

Aedh looked across the water to the distant shore. 'But it's so far away,' he complained. 'It's a long way to row.'

'Well, if you all get into the boat,' Lir said, 'I'll show you a little magic of my own.' And, when they were all safely seated in the small round boat, Lir pushed it out into the lake and jumped in. He then leaned over and dipped his hand in the water and moved his fingers to and fro in a strange way. The calm waters suddenly swelled behind them and a large wave formed beneath the boat and carried it swiftly and smoothly to the far shore.

Chapter Three

'My father soon began meeting Aife every day, and it soon became clear to Aedh and me that he was in love with her. It didn't really come as any surprise when our father took the four of us down to the lakeside one evening and told us that he was going to ask Aife to marry him.

' "But what about mother . . .?" I asked.

' "I think Eva would approve," our father said quietly, "and I don't think she would want you to grow up without a mother."

' "Well, I'll never forget her," Aedh said quickly, and I saw tears sparkling in his eyes.

'Our father knelt down on the soft earth and gathered us both into his arms. "I don't want you to forget her. She is, and always will be, your mother, but now . . ." he paused. "But now you will have a second mother, a stepmother." '

'My father married Aife a short time after that. They were married according to the ancient customs in the middle of a forest, and all the lords and ladies of the Tuatha De Danann attended.

'I was Aife's bridesmaid, and Fiachra and Conn carried the train of her long shimmering silver gown, while Aedh walked before her, carrying our father's sword of silver-blue coral. The wedding was a huge happy event, and there was feasting and merry-making for three whole days afterwards.

'And then we returned to the White Fort with our new stepmother, and she quickly set about making the palace a place to live in once again.

A Warning

'She had the white walls scoured clean and then painted with bright new paint that one of the old women in the village made from berries and the bark of certain trees. The roof was then cleaned and twenty men, with their helpers, worked for more than twenty days just scraping the muck off the gold tiles, and digging out the tufts of grass that had taken root there.

'Soon the White Fort began to look as lovely as it had always been.

'In those early days, shortly after she was married, Aife was kind and gentle and treated us as if we were her own children. However, as the months passed, she began to change towards us. At first it was just in little ways; things we would do or say would anger her for no reason, and I sometimes found her looking at us in a strange way, in a way that frightened me.

'It was almost a year from the time she had married our father before we discovered why she had come to hate us so . . .'

Fionnuala stood beneath the apple tree with Fiachra and Conn by her side. They were watching Aedh, who was up in the very highest branches of the tree, carefully untangling Conn's kite which had blown into it.

'Be careful,' Fionnuala said quietly, afraid that a shout might startle her brother and perhaps make him fall.

'Yes,' Conn called up to his older brother, 'it's a new

kite and I don't want it broken or torn.'

Aedh laughed and dropped a small unripened apple down on to his brother's head. He pulled another one free and was just about to drop it when he stopped and the laughter froze in his throat. He was looking across the field and his brothers and sister followed the direction of his gaze and turned around. Aife was hurrying towards them.

When Fionnuala saw who it was, she started to smile and half-raised her hand in a wave, but then she stopped when she saw the expression on her stepmother's face. It was cold and hard and angry. Conn took hold of one of his sister's hands, while Fiachra held on to the other.

Aife strode through the little orchard along the muddy path, her high, doeskin boots sinking into the soft earth, and the hem of her long gown trailing in the muck. She stopped in front of the children, and put her hands on her hips. She was shaking and white-faced with rage and made two attempts to speak before her voice came out without trembling.

'Just what do you think you're doing?' she demanded angrily.

'Why, nothing . . .' Aedh began.

'Nothing!' she snapped. 'Nothing. I have told you before not to come into this orchard. I have told you not to climb the trees. And yet, here you are, disobeying both my commands. And not only that, but you're also destroying the fruit.'

'I only climbed up to get . . .' Aedh started to say, but Aife cut him short.

'I will not listen to any excuses. You can all return to your rooms, and I do not want to see you again before tomorrow morning.'

'But what about supper . . .' Fiachra said quietly.

'You will get no supper,' Aife snapped. 'You should have thought about that before.' She turned on her heel and marched back along the path towards the palace.

The four children watched her disappear and then Fiachra began to cry softly. Fionnuala held and comforted him, although she very much felt like crying herself; it was so unfair, they had not been doing anything wrong.

Aedh freed Conn's kite and lowered it down to him by the tangled string, and then they set out for their Fort. They took a different path to the one their stepmother had taken, so that they wouldn't meet her, one that would bring them in by the kitchens.

On their way through the kitchen gardens they met Mechar, their father's servant. He stopped when he saw their woeful expressions, and Fiachra's red eyes. Stooping down, he lifted up the twins in his strong arms. 'What's the matter with you, eh?' he asked, his usually rough voice now soft and concerned.

'Our stepmother spoke harshly to us,' Conn said with a sniffle. 'And she has sent us to bed with no supper,' he added.

'And . . . and for no reason,' his twin said with a stammer. 'We . . . we were doing nothing.'

'You must have been doing something wrong,' Mechar said, looking at the two older children.

Aedh quickly explained what had happened and Fionnuala nodded. 'She seemed to get upset over nothing.'

Mechar's expression changed and he put the twins down. 'Why don't you run along into the kitchen,' he suggested. 'I think Mairid made some honey and nut cakes earlier on.'

'Honey and nut...'

'Our favourites...'

And the twins were off, racing down the path towards the kitchen door, their upset already forgotten.

Mechar watched them go with a slight smile on his lips and then he turned back to the two older children. 'Why don't we walk in your mother's garden?' he said softly.

Aedh and Fionnuala followed the tall figure out into the small garden that was set apart from the kitchen and herb gardens by a high wall. Aife had forbidden them to enter this garden, too. It had been their mother's private garden and her special pride and joy, and she had spent many afternoons tending to the trees and flowers that travellers brought her from the four corners of the world. In the height of summer it was usually a mass of colour and you could almost taste the many strange scents on the air.

But now, however, at a time when everything should have been in full bloom, it was overrun with weeds and nettles and tall grasses grew between the flowerbeds and choked the little stream and artificial lake. All the beautifully carved statues were lost, hidden behind bushes and entangled amongst branches.

Fionnuala felt tears sting her eyes when she remembered how carefully her mother had kept this little garden, and how disappointed she would be if she saw it now. But Aife had no interest in flowers and gardening, and the children were not even allowed in here, so they couldn't clean it up themselves.

Mechar led them along a path. A small tree had fallen across it and they had to climb over it to reach the tiny lake that lay in the very centre of the garden. Mechar stopped by the side of the still water, his head bowed and his hands buried in his large sleeves.

'I have been with your father for many years,' he said suddenly, startling both children, making them jump. 'I was by his side when we sailed on our ships of metal and magic from our enchanted cities across the sea to this green and fertile land.' He smiled suddenly. 'You may not know this, but he and I are cousins of sorts, and so you and I are also related.' He turned around and stood with his back to the water, staring down at the boy and girl. 'I have always thought of you as my own children and, if I have ever been harsh with you, it was only to keep you from harm. I have never been cruel to you, have I?' he asked, and they both shook their heads. 'You know I have fought in many, many battles and have defeated giants and demons, and you know that I fear nothing?' They nodded again. 'But now, children, I am frightened. Oh, not for myself, but for you, for all of you.'

'But why, Mechar?' Fionnuala asked in a whisper.

'This has something to do with our stepmother, hasn't it?' Aedh asked.

Mechar nodded. 'Your stepmother went to see the wise woman in the village today,' he began slowly. 'She asked the old witch-woman if she would ever bear your father any children. The answer was "no".' Mechar saw their looks of puzzlement and continued. 'You see, according to the law, the four of you – the children of Lir – will inherit your father's land and fortune when he decides he no longer wishes to rule, or when the long Sleep comes on him. However, if Aife were to have a child, then that child would be the heir, and would get everything. You would get nothing.'

'And Aife was told she would never have any children,' Aedh said. 'It's no wonder she was so angry.'

'I know it's very sad that she should be childless,' Fionnuala said, 'but she does have us . . . and why should that make you frightened for us?'

'I fear that since she can have no children of her own, she might just decide that there should be no children at all to inherit Lir's fortune!'

Aedh and Fionnuala looked at him in horror; what he was saying was . . . impossible.

'But we are De Danann, we cannot be killed,' Aedh protested.

Mechar shook his head. 'Of course you can be killed. All that would happen is that your ghosts would not rest until your murderer had been caught and punished. But you would be very much dead, I'm afraid, and no amount of magic would be able to bring you back.'

Fionnuala, who had pulled a dead leaf off a tree and had been twirling it between her fingers, suddenly threw the remains on to the green-scummed water of the lake. 'But surely that would stop her from killing us. I mean, surely she knows she would be found out.'

The tall man nodded. 'That's true. But she could have you kidnapped and taken to the four corners of the world,' he said quickly, 'and what would you do then? All I'm asking you to do is to be extra careful, especially when your stepmother is around. Promise me?' he asked softly.

The boy and girl looked at one another and nodded their heads. What Mechar had said had frightened them.

Mechar then reached into the pouch that he carried on his belt and pulled out two small black stones. There was a small circular hole through the centre of each stone, and there was a thin leather string looped through it. He hung the stones around the children's necks by the cord.

'You must promise me that you will wear these always,' he insisted. 'These are the Stones of Truth; they are older than the Tuatha De Danann, and are touched with the First Magic ever to come into this world. Wear them and I will always know where to find you.' He stood up and smiled. 'I have to go now,' he said, and turned and made his way back though the overgrown garden towards the kitchens.

Aedh and Fionnuala stood and watched him disappear through the trees, and when he was gone they turned and stared into the still green waters of the stagnant lake. The stones around their necks felt cold and heavy, and only reminded them that their stepmother wished them harm.

A bubble burst on the thick green water, and the sudden plop made them both jump, and set their hearts pounding. They shivered then, although it was not a cold evening . . .

Chapter Four

'From that day on our stepmother was very cruel and harsh towards us. We could do nothing right and she said that we did wrong just to annoy and upset her.

'We were no longer allowed to go swimming in the lakes and streams; we were no longer allowed to climb the trees or wander along the corridors of our father's Fort, and we were forbidden to go out into the gardens.

'She often spoke to our father about us, but he loved us very deeply and would hear nothing bad said about us, and told her that she must be imagining things. And Aife hated us all the more for that, and I suppose she believed that he loved us more than he loved her – which was not true, because he loved her very deeply.

'Aife then fell ill – or she said that she was ill, because when our father sent the best doctors and wizards to see her, they could find nothing wrong and said that it was either an imagined sickness, or else a sickness of the mind rather than the body.

'Our stepmother, however, insisted that she was sick, and so she kept to her bed in a darkened room, and had all her food sent up to her. She refused to see us, for she said that we made her feel worse and were noisy, and gave her a headache. She rarely saw our father and he spent a lot of time either hunting or in the Tir faoi Thuinn, the Land Beneath the Waves. She spent a whole year in bed without getting up once!

'And then one day when our father was away with his men

Enchanted

hunting down a wild boar that was destroying the crops and killing the farm animals in the southern part of his kingdom, Aifef"recovered" . . .'

Everything seemed to fall silent when Aife appeared in the courtyard of the White Fort. The Queen hadn't been seen in over a year; she was supposed to be dreadfully ill and close to death – true death, that is, and not the long-lasting sleep of the De Danann people. Even the De Danann folk could die if they neither ate nor drank or if they ate and drank far too much, and Aife was supposed to be overeating and drinking.

Fionnuala and Aedh looked up as the tall shadow fell across them. They were sitting on one of the lower steps that led up to the great hallway, playing a board game with twigs and stones, moving the pieces to and fro, winning and losing them again. When they saw their stepmother, they quickly scrambled to their feet, their game forgotten.

They were both shocked not only at seeing the Queen again, but the change that had come over her during her year in bed. She had put on a lot of weight, and her lovely heart-shaped face had grown puffy, there were now bags under her eyes and she had a double-chin. There were fine threads of silver and grey in her hair, which was no longer quite so thick and shining as it had once been.

Aedh was the first to recover from the shock of seeing his stepmother again. 'My lady ... are you well?' he asked quickly.

'I am somewhat recovered, thank you,' Aife said coldly, and her thin lips moved in a quick icy smile.

'Has your illness passed?' Fionnuala asked.

Aife walked slowly down the steps, casually kicking their board game out of her way. 'It has gone for a little time, I think.' She smiled again, and then breathed deeply. 'However, I think I shall soon be rid of it for ever,' she added in a strange voice, and this time her smile was frightening. She walked past the children and out into the centre of the small courtyard, and then she stopped and looked back over her shoulder. 'I found I could not stay in bed on this lovely morning. I think it would be the perfect day to visit your grandfather,' she added. 'We can bring a picnic with us. What do you think?' Without waiting for an answer, she turned away and strode across the courtyard, calling for the servants to prepare her chariot and to make up a picnic.

The boy and girl stood quietly watching her, and when she had disappeared into the kitchen, Aedh turned to his older sister. 'What do you think?' he asked.

Fionnuala shook her head, her thick dark hair shimmering green in the sunlight. 'I don't like it,' she said quietly, 'it seems so sudden.'

'But what are we going to do?' he wondered.

'Well ... we can't disobey her. We'll have to go.' She frowned and rubbed the stone which still hung around her neck.

'I'll tell you what,' Aedh said, 'you go and find Conn and Fiachra – I'm sure I saw them going into the stables to look at the new ponies – and while you're doing that, I'll go and tell Mechar. He will know what to do.'

'Tell him to send a message by one of his trained golden eagles to Bov's Fort, warning them to expect us,' Fionnuala said.

Aedh nodded. 'That's a good idea.' He ran across the courtyard and up the steps heading for Mechar's rooms. At least if they told him, someone would know where they were going. Fionnuala stood on the steps for a moment, before finally sighing and turning away towards the stables. For some strange reason she felt very lonely and frightened.

Aife returned with her chariot a little while later. It was shaped something like a big basket, open at one end, and had four hard wooden wheels. It was pulled by four horses. The chariot was driven by Donn, one of the servants she had brought with her from her father's court. He was a tall blond-haired and blue-eyed foreigner from one of the lands that lay far to the east of Banba, and he would not – or could not – speak. He also took orders only from Aife.

Fionnuala, Aedh, Conn and Fiachra were waiting by the huge wooden gates of the Fort when Donn came galloping out from the direction of the stables at the back of the palace. He saw the children and pulled hard on the reins. Turning the chariot sharply in a tight circle, he sent a shower of dust up and over the four children as he stopped.

Aife helped them up on to the wood-and-wicker chariot, and then gave a signal to Donn. He drew back his long whip and cracked it over the horses' heads, and the chariot jolted forward. Donn cracked the whip again, and the four animals picked up speed, and soon they were going as fast as possible, sliding around sharp bends and bouncing over the ruts in the rough road. The four children clung tightly to the sides of the chariot and soon both Conn and Fiachra began to look pale and frightened.

Aedh touched his stepmother's arm, and shouted at her above the whipping breeze and the rumble of the hard wooden wheels. 'We must stop; my brothers are feeling sick!'

Aife looked back at the twins and then she nodded. She leaned over and touched Donn on the shoulder and then pointed to where the gleam of water could be seen through the trees and bushes. The charioteer immediately pulled on the right-hand rein and the horses veered away from the road and bounced over the hard earth, leaving long tracks in the grass that was still damp from the morning's dew. He drove straight through bushes, sending startled birds up into the clear blue sky, and disturbing a rabbit which bounded half-way across the field, before it stopped and stood on its hind legs to watch them with button-bright eyes.

The charioteer finally pulled the horses to a stop close to the edge of a lake. Aedh immediately jumped out and helped his two brothers to the ground and then Fionnuala. The four of them walked down on to the small sandy beach beside the water, glad to be back on solid ground again.

'Don't go too far,' Aife called after them. 'We'll picnic here and afterwards we must hurry on. I want to reach Bov's Fort by noon.'

The four children stood by the water's edge and stared

out across the still blue-green waters of the lake. Conn and Fiachra were looking a little better. 'He was going so fast,' Conn complained, 'and all that bouncing around was making me feel sick.'

'Me too,' Fiachra agreed.

Aife hurried up after them, her wooden-soled sandals crunching on the sand. 'The picnic will be ready in a few moments; Donn is just spreading it out.' The Queen took a deep breath and looked out across the waters of the lake. 'It's such a lovely day, why don't you go in for a swim,' she suggested. 'We'll eat when you're finished.'

Aedh glanced across at Fionnuala and she nodded; there was nothing Aife could do while they were swimming, was there?

They quickly stripped off and dived into the water. It was ice cold and they gasped with the shock, but then the gills in their throats opened and they didn't have to swallow any of the water. They swam easily, like fishes, with their arms close to their sides, twisting and turning by using tiny movements of their feet. However, the water was so cold that they soon decided it was time to finish, and besides, they were getting hungry.

The four heads broke the surface of the water together. From the distance they looked like seals, sleek and shining. They began to swim towards the shore, the palms of their hands flat against their legs, their feet moving very quickly. They swam silently, with no splashing. As they neared the small, rough beach they noticed that Aife and Donn were nowhere to be seen. They stopped swimming and bobbed in the chill water; where was she? Had she perhaps driven off and left them? They hesitated for a few moments, and then Fionnuala said, 'Well, we can't stay here for ever, can we?' and she kicked off with her legs and then allowed the current to pull her in close to the shore.

They were wading through the shallow water when Aife reappeared. She must have been standing behind a tree watching them, waiting for them to come near to the shore. The first thing the children noticed was that she had changed her clothes, and she was no longer dressed in her gown of green and gold. Now she wore a long gown of midnight black, edged around the throat and hem with broad bands of deep red that had matched the red streaks in her hair. There was a strange twisting design in this band that had been picked out in bright golden thread. But what made the four children stop and stare at her in fright and curiosity was that she was also wearing a long flowing dark cloak which glittered and shimmered with strange designs.

And the children of Lir knew that the De Danann people only wore these ancient cloaks when they were going to work some powerful magic.

Something about the cloak was familiar and then Fionnuala suddenly realized what it was. She pointed, her mouth opening into an 'O' of surprise. 'That's our father's magical cloak.'

Aife strode down the beach in a few quick steps. She was barefoot now and she barely made a sound on the rough sand and pebbles. She smiled, a cold, frightening smile.

'Yes, this is your father's cloak. This cloak is woven from the mists of morning and the dew of evening, from the first shafts of sunlight and the last rays of twilight. The foam of the sea spray and the fresh salt smells have gone into it, and it is made up out of the strength of a sea storm and the gentleness of a sea breeze.' Aife spun around suddenly and the cloak twirled about her, and then she held up a part of it in her hands. 'It is the most powerful magical cloak in these islands.'

'Why are you wearing it, stepmother?' Aedh asked quietly.

Aife leaned forward and her hard eyes narrowed. 'Because I need its strength,' she said. 'I am going to work the most powerful magic that has been worked in this land since it was first made.'

'And what magic is that?' Fionnuala whispered.

Their stepmother took another step forward and smiled again, showing her small pointed teeth. 'For far too long you have stood between me and your father; I know he loves you much more than he loves me. Every time he looks at you, he is reminded of my sister, your mother. So . . . now I am going to remove you,' her voice had dropped to a whisper and the four children had to strain to hear her.

'You cannot kill us,' Aedh said. 'We are the children of Lir, of the tribe of the Tuatha De Danann. If you kill us our ghosts will rise and haunt you, and everyone will know what you have done.'

Aife nodded. 'Oh, I know that. No, I am not going to kill you, I am not so foolish.' She paused and whirled the shimmering, glittering cloak around her once more. 'Oh no, not kill you – I am going to change you!'

And before the four children could move, Aife made a strange shape in the air with the fingers of her left hand and they suddenly found that they were frozen to the spot, unable to move.

Aife took her time then. She first broke a branch off a nearby alder tree and changed it into a shining black wand almost half as tall as herself. She splashed out into the shallows and walked anti-clockwise around the four children with the point of her wand splashing through the water. She then stood back and spoke a word, and the circle glowed red and gold on the water. Aife turned back and then threw the wand high into the air. The children saw it shatter into a fine cloud of dust which scattered on the light breeze.

Their stepmother then pulled the magical cloak tightly around her shoulders and bent her head. They could see that her forehead was wrinkled with strain and her eyes squeezed tightly shut. Her lips were moving quickly, but no sound came out except for a faint buzzing, like an angry trapped bee. And then slowly, slowly, slowly, Aife raised her head and opened her eyes. They were glowing with a reddish fire from within. She smiled and then spread the cloak wide with both arms. The strange intricate and beautiful designs on the inside of the cloak began to glow and shine, and soon the entire cloak was a sheet of pounding light which blinded the four children.

And then the light flowed off the cloak and rolled along the ground in a huge ball. It hissed a little as it moved leaving behind it a trail of burnt and crisped grass and hardened sand. When it touched the water it exploded into steam which rose up in a thick dense fog. The children of Lir felt the hot steam tingling along their legs and arms. The tingling grew stronger until it felt like pins and needles, and then they found that they could no longer feel their feet . . . and then their legs . . . thighs . . . stomachs . . . chests . . . arms . . . necks . . . heads . . .

For one terrible moment they went deaf and blind.

When they could see again, they found that Aife had grown huge and towered over them like a giantess. Aedh shouted in rage and tried to jump forward. He felt

his arms moving, but nothing happened, except that water splashed in every direction. He looked around for his sister and brothers ... and then he cried aloud in horror and terror.

For Fionnuala, Conn and Fiachra were gone, and in their places three snow-white swans floated on the still waters of the lake. Aedh looked down into the water at his own reflection ... and the small, delicate head of a swan looked back up at him!

Chapter Five

'Our stepmother had changed us into swans. She then put a spell on us so that we would remain in the shape of birds for nine hundred years, and even then we would not return to our own shape until we heard a church bell ringing in the evening stillness. And you must remember that in those days there were no such things as churches or bells in Banba, so we didn't even know what she was talking about.

'She had also put a geasa – which is a special sort of spell which makes you do something you don't want to – on us so that we would have to spend the first three hundred years on the lake we were in, which was called Lough Derravaragh; the second three hundred in the icy waters of the Straits of Moyle, which lies between Banba and Alba, and the last three hundred in the waters around the island of Inish Glora, which lies off the western coast. And, as I say, to complete the spell, we would have to hear the bell of the New God.

'However, even though Aife could rob us of our human shapes, she could not take away our voices, and we could still speak perfectly.

'And so we floated there on the cold water of the lake, feeling the wind ruffling our feathers, and watched our stepmother ride away with her charioteer, and she was laughing.

'We wondered what would happen to her; we wondered what would happen to us . . .'

The Just Reward

The chariot had just disappeared over the brow of a hill in a cloud of dust when a single horseman came riding around a bend in the road in the opposite direction – the same one from which the children had come only a short time ago. He rode slowly, with one hand on the reins, and the other held out before him, holding something which dangled from a string.

The rider paused by the road and then he urged his horse across the fields towards the waters of the lake. He dismounted and pushed his way through the bushes, now following the tracks the chariot wheels had made through the tall grass.

The four children of Lir drifted silently into the tall rushes that grew up by the side of the lake and hid there, wondering who the rider was. Their eyesight had changed when they had become swans, it was sharper and harder and clearer, but, because they were so close to the ground, they couldn't see as much.

The tall bulky man crunched down on to the sand and then he paused by the water's edge. He lifted up his left hand. The children could see a strange pointed stone turning on the end of a long leather cord. The stone swung and shifted and then turned to point directly towards the reeds where the children were hiding. The tall man stepped closer to the reeds and pushed back the hood of the long grey cloak he was wearing.

'It's Mechar,' Aedh said suddenly recognizing the figure. He pushed his way out of the reeds and drifted over to their friend.

Mechar frowned when he saw the beautiful snow-white bird drift out of the reeds and move silently towards him. He looked down at the magic stone in his hand: it was now pointing directly towards the swan.

But it should be pointing towards the children. Where were the children?

He had waited until the four of them had gone with Aife and then, when the chariot had rounded the turn in the road, he had set out to follow it. His direction-stone pointed the way, because it was the twin of the stones which he had given Aedh and Fionnuala, and it would always point to them.

And so he was puzzled now. Why did the stone in his hand point towards this tall, beautiful swan? The large bird came up and rubbed its slender head against his hand. Mechar was amazed, for swans were usually the shyest of birds, and yet could be terribly fierce if a man came too close to them. There was a sudden movement in the reeds and then three more swans, one large and two smaller ones, moved slowly towards him.

And Mechar suddenly knew what had happened!

He fell to his knees in the cold water and looked closely at the four birds. He looked into their eyes and he knew them: Aedh and Fionnuala, Conn and Fiachra, the twins. He knew then what Aife had done, and he knew also that he had to reach Bov's Fort before she did.

Mechar stroked their heads gently, and there were tears in his eyes. 'There is nothing I can do for you now,' he said softly, 'but I will find your father, and I'll tell Bov what his daughter has done. He should know how to reverse the spell. I'm sure he will be able to return you to your own shapes.'

'I don't think anything can help us now,' the tallest swan, Aedh, said. 'You know that De Danann magic is the most powerful in the world and that once made it cannot be undone.'

Mechar almost fell backwards with fright. 'You can talk!'

'Aife has changed our shapes and placed us under a nine-hundred-year enchantment, but she could not take our voices,' the second swan said, and Mechar recognized Fionnuala's voice.

'What will Aife do now?' Aedh asked, his feathers ruffling in the breeze that blew across the lake.

'She will probably go on to her father's Fort, and tell them some story about the four of you being kidnapped by bandits or eaten by wolves.' He shrugged. 'I'm sure she would make it a good story.' He smiled coldly and stood up. 'But what she does not know is that I've sent on a messenger-bird, and in the message I told your grandfather to expect you later on this morning. But I've also asked Bov not to listen to any tale Aife might tell if she arrives without you. My messenger-eagle will also warn the King that I suspect that your stepmother might try to harm you.'

'What will you do now?' Aedh asked.

'I'm going to ride on to Bov's Fort to tell them what has happened here.'

'Bring our father back with you,' Conn said, and there were tears in his eyes and a catch in his voice as he asked.

'Oh, I will,' Mechar promised, 'I will.'

When Mechar reached Bov's Fort, he found the place in an uproar. He questioned some of the guards on the gate, who knew him, and found out that Aife had ridden in a little earlier, alone and in great distress.

The Queen had told how she had been on the way to her father's fort with her four stepchildren and her charioteer, Donn. On the way the children had complained of the heat and so they had stopped at Lough Derravaragh. But on the beach, the children had been attacked by wild boars – huge pigs with razor-sharp teeth and tusks – and although she and Donn had fought the animals and attempted to save the children, one by one they had been killed and eaten by the boars. She also said that Donn had fallen to their snarling tusks.

Mechar listened in amazement. It was a very clever story, since it meant that there were no bodies to account for, and it also looked as if she were a heroine who had fought bravely in defence of her stepchildren. He smiled grimly and wondered what she had done with the charioteer; probably used her magic power to turn him into something – a snail, a moth or a small bird, he guessed.

Mechar hurried through the palace, down the long corridors where the guards were rushing to and fro, gathering together a hunting party to go in search of the boars. He found Aife in the throne-room with Lir and her father, Bov. Mechar strode in through the tall door without knocking or announcing himself and they all stopped talking.

Lir took a few steps towards him. Mechar could see that the King was terribly upset, and he suddenly seemed older. 'You've heard . . .' he began.

Mechar nodded. 'I know, my lord,' he said softly, and then he paused and added in a loud angry voice. 'I know the truth about what has happened, my lord.'

Bov looked up at the loud voice. 'What do you mean, you know the truth,' he demanded, his hard green eyes boring right through the younger man.

Mechar looked at him in astonishment. 'Didn't you get my message?' he asked.

Bov nodded slowly. 'Aye, I received that strange message saying that you suspected my daughter might try to harm the children.' He paused and added in a different tone, glancing across at his daughter, 'I had forgotten about it in all the excitement.'

All the colour drained from Aife's face, and she suddenly looked frightened. 'What nonsense!' she snapped. 'I did everything in my power to protect them.' Tears came into her eyes and her voice broke. 'But the boars were so ferocious . . .'

'Where did the boars attack you?' Mechar asked quietly, his voice hard and dangerous.

'On the banks of Lough Derravaragh,' Aife said quickly. 'The children were swimming, and just as they were coming out of the water, the boars attacked. There were dozens of them and they must have been waiting in the bushes.' She hung her head and began crying again. 'My charioteer died defending them.'

Mechar took a step forward. 'Tell me,' he asked quietly, 'why didn't you change the wild boars into something else? Your power is transformation, isn't it – well, why didn't you use it?'

Lir looked at his wife. 'Yes, Aife, why didn't you do that?'

The Queen looked quickly from Mechar to Lir and then turned back to her father. 'There was no time; it all happened so quickly.'

Even Bov was looking at her strangely now, and he turned back to Mechar without saying a word to her. 'What are you saying, young man?' he demanded.

'I have just come from Lough Derravaragh,' Mechar said, his voice dropping to a whisper, but in the silent throne-room they could hear him clearly enough. 'There are four swans on the waters of the lake; four beautiful, snow-white swans. But these are not ordinary swans, oh no,' he shook his head, 'for these birds can talk. They are the children of Lir!' He paused and added softly, 'They have been changed into swans by that woman there!' He pointed directly towards the Queen.

Aife attempted to laugh, but all that came out was a choking sound. She shook her head from side to side. 'Oh no, it's not true, it's not true, I never . . .'

Mechar stepped closer to the pale-faced woman. 'You

used your magical power to change them into swans,' he accused, 'and you have placed them under a nine-hundred-year enchantment.'

'It's a lie,' Aife screamed. 'He hates me, he's always hated me. He's only saying this because he hates me . . .'

Mechar smiled sadly and shook his head. He looked at Bov and Lir. 'Ride to Derravaragh and see for yourselves.'

Bov suddenly stood up and roared for a servant. When the man came scurrying up, the King told him to bring the Mirror of Truth. The frightened servant hurried away. He had never seen the King looking so angry before: his hair and beard almost bristled, his face was red and his eyes were like chips of green ice.

When the servant returned a few moments later with the mirror, he found Aife screaming and shouting, first at her husband and then at her father, while a third man, whom the servant knew to be one of Lir's personal servants and friends, stood quietly by, a look of terrible sorrow on his broad face.

Bov took the magic mirror and dismissed the servant. The King carefully removed the black and red silk cloth that covered it, and then he held the glass up in front of Aife. It was almost as large as a shield, with a beautiful, intricately-designed golden frame. But the glass itself was black: it reflected nothing.

'Look into the mirror, daughter,' Bov commanded, 'and tell me once again what happened. Remember,' he warned her, 'this is the Mirror of Truth, you cannot lie to it.'

Aife began her story once again, and as she spoke a picture formed in the black glass. But it was not a picture of the children being attacked by a pack of wild pigs, rather it was the image of Aife standing by the water's edge dressed in a magical cloak and using her spells to transform the children into four swans. It showed her riding away with Donn, and then it showed her changing the charioteer into a tiny, rainbow-winged fly as they neared Bov's Fort. When she had finished, the colours and shapes on the mirror swirled and gradually turned once more to black.

Bov's anger was terrible. He had loved his grandchildren dearly, and was horrified to think that his daughter, their stepmother, could do such a terrible thing to them. He turned away from her without saying a word, and walked back to his throne of red stone. He picked up his crown and sceptre and sat down. After a few moments he put the high golden crown on his head and then lifted the sceptre high. He spoke an ancient word and the short length of beaten gold turned into a plain wooden wand.

'You have done a terrible thing, my daughter,' he said coldly, pointing the wand at her. 'You have shamed me and this noble house, and by doing so, you have shamed all the people of the Tuatha De Danann. You are no longer welcome in my house, and no longer can you be part of the People of the Goddess.' As he spoke he began to move the wand in a strange pattern in the air.

'You have taken away my grandchildren's human form, and so I too, will take away yours.'

Bov moved the wand again and a sudden cold breeze blew through the throne-room. Aife began to shiver, although neither Lir nor Mechar felt the terrible cold she was now feeling. A thin covering of ice formed on her hair and eyelashes, and her pale skin turned blue with the cold. Soon she was completely covered with a pale

thin covering of ice, and then it began to thicken and harden, and soon Aife could no longer be seen within the solid block of ice.

Bov then whispered another word and a thin line of bright green fire shot from the tip of the wand and darted towards the block of ice. It struck the surface of the block and began to fizz and hiss, and then it shot to and fro, darting and spinning and wherever it touched, the ice began to melt. When it had completely covered the block and all the ice was beginning to run, the green fire darted back into the wand.

The three men stood silently waiting for the ice to melt. And when it did, they found Aife had disappeared.

Lir stepped forward into the spreading pool of water and poked amongst the lumps of half-frozen ice and then he pulled out a small, long-tailed, shining-eyed lizard. The creature opened its mouth and hissed, and a forked tongue flickered back and forth. It hissed again and then unfolded a pair of almost transparent wings and flapped upwards. It circled once around the small silent group, hissing all the time, and then it headed out through the open window.

There was a sudden flapping of wings and Mechar's huge golden messenger-eagle darted past the window, its long claws extended, reaching for the lizard. It opened its beak and screeched hungrily. When it flew past the window again, something dangled from its claws.

Aife had received her just reward.

Chapter Six

'And so we began the first three hundred years of our enchantment on the cold waters of Lough Derravaragh.

'Our father and grandfather and the greatest wizards and magicians in all the known world came and tried to turn us back into our human forms, but no one succeeded. Aife had set the spell in a certain way, a way that only she could undo, and of course, she was now gone. We were trapped.

'Our father moved his court to the banks of the lake, and the finest scholars and teachers in the world came and taught us. We learned many things, but most of all, we learned to sing. And soon our music and songs became known through the length and breadth of Banba. People came from miles around just to hear us sing.

'There was a certain magic in our voices, and if we sang sad songs, nearly everybody cried, but if we sang happy songs, then everyone laughed and smiled.

'But the first three hundred years soon passed. We did not feel the time slipping by, but one morning I woke up and I just knew that we had to leave. We hadn't aged, but our father had . . .'

The Straits of Moyle

Lir had grown old as he lived by the waters of Lough Derravaragh. His green hair was now streaked with silver and there were lines on his forehead and about his eyes. He stood on the sandy banks of the lake and watched the four swans – his children – glide silently across the water towards him. The old man shaded his eyes and squinted into the morning mist which still clung to the water, and watched them come closer. At one time, when he was younger, and his sight was clearer than it was now, he would have been able to tell one from the other even from the other side of the lake. But now . . . he smiled sadly; he should have taken the long Sleep of the De Danann people long ago, but he had hung on, wanting to be close to his children, and now he was ageing like the human people.

One of the swans swam right up to the edge of the water and Lir's old eyes filled with tears as he recognized it. 'My son,' he said in a whisper.

'Father . . .' Aedh bowed his long slender neck, but couldn't say any more.

A second swan joined them, and Lir recognized Fionnuala's bright eyes even before he heard her sweet voice. 'Father,' she began, 'we must leave this lake today; the first part of our enchantment is over, and now we must head north to the wild waters of Moyle.'

The old King nodded. 'I know,' he said. 'I have

watched the years come and go. I have watched my friends and servants grow old and tired and go into the secret resting places of the De Danann people – soon I will have to follow them.' He paused and shook his head sadly. 'Soon, my children, none of the People of the Goddess will be left in Banba, we will all be Sleeping. It will be many years before we will come again.' There were tears in his eyes as he looked across the cold grey waters of the lake. 'When you go now, I will be alone,' he said.

'You will have Mechar,' Aedh said.

Lir shook his head. 'Mechar fell into the long Sleep last night,' he whispered. 'There is no one left here but me.'

The four children looked around at the Fort and the town that had grown up around it – and he was right. There was no movement, no sounds, no smoke from the morning fires, no dogs barking. The town was deserted. All the De Danann people had gone.

'Father,' Fionnuala said softly, feeling the strong pull of the curse, 'we must go now.'

'What will happen to you?' Conn asked, very quietly.

'I will Sleep in the Tir faoi Thuinn,' his father said with a smile, 'but don't you worry, I will come again.' Lir then knelt in the sand and, as each swan came up to him, he bent and kissed the top of its silken head. The four swans then drifted out into the centre of the lake, until they were almost lost in the fog, and then they flapped their huge wings and began to beat their way across the water. The morning mists billowed and curled about them like smoke and then they were up in the air, their wings beating strongly. They strung out in a line, with Fionnuala in the lead, Aedh behind her and Conn and Fiachra following, and then they swung around in a tight circle over the lake. They sang an ancient song of parting, full of sorrow and heartbreak which echoed over the land, and people who heard it felt the tears come to their eyes. Even the birds and animals fell silent as the haunting music filled the air.

The four swans then turned towards the north and, with the wind in their faces, they set out for the Straits of Moyle. And the last they ever saw of their father was a sad old man standing tall and proud by the waters of Lough Derravaragh with tears on his face.

The four swans flew northwards for most of the morning. They flew over lakes and rivers, mountains and huge forests – for in those days most of the land was covered with trees. Once or twice they passed the shining towers of a De Danann Fort, and they saw the tall figures standing on the battlements waving up at them, for everyone in Banba knew the children of Lir: they had become a legend in their own lifetime.

About noon they passed over the barren northern cliffs and soon they were out over the Straits of Moyle where they would spend the second stage of their nine-hundred-year enchantment. They dropped downwards on to the grey sea and settled on a barren outcrop of rock, exhausted after their long flight.

All around them there was nothing but a flat expanse of cold grey-green sea. The water was freezing and there were even tiny chunks of ice which had floated down from the frozen northern seas. A chill wind blew down from the north and sometimes a stronger gust blew in rain and sleet on the four shivering birds.

They remained on the tiny rock all day, while all around them the wind and sea rose and low dark clouds rolled across an angry sky.

'There's a storm coming,' Aedh said, shouting above the wind which had started to howl.

'The first of many, I think,' Fionnuala said. 'The seas around here are always rough and stormy, even in the middle of summer.'

'What are we going to do?' Aedh asked, sounding worried.

'We must try to stay together,' Fionnuala said. 'We'll make this rock our base, and if the storm separates us, we must try to return to it . . .'

She had barely finished speaking when a huge wave washed in over the barren rock and when it had passed, the four swans were gone, swept away into the wild and stormy sea.

The storm lasted nearly three days and three nights. It rained snow and ice, and the wind blowing down from the arctic north was as sharp as a knife and bitterly cold. Thunder and lightning rolled across the skies and the lightning flashes turned the night into day.

The four swans were roughly tossed about in all directions. Fionnuala and Aedh managed to stay together for a little while, and once they passed very close to another white swan, which might have been Conn, although the bird had come and gone so quickly that it was hard to tell. However, after a terrific peal of thunder and a jagged streak of lightning that seemed to tear the sky in half, Fionnuala and her brother became separated and now each of the four swans was alone on the wild waves.

Fionnuala was the first to reach the barren outcrop of rock they had chosen as their base. She was bruised and battered, cold and terribly hungry. She was also very tired, but the first thing she did was to climb to the highest point on the rock and look about her in every direction, searching for her missing brothers. The sun had not yet risen, although the sky was beginning to brighten, and she could see clearly enough. But the grey sea was flat and empty.

She remained there for the rest of the morning, watching and waiting. The sea was a little calmer, although the occasional wave still washed over the rock and she had to struggle to keep her footing on the slippery rock. But the storm was over – although far to the south there were still grey clouds, and she guessed it would be raining now over Banba.

As the day wore on she began to sing. She sang in her

strong clear voice that carried out over the waves in every direction. She sang the songs she had learned as a child; she sang the songs she and Aedh had both taught to the twins, and she sang of the Tuatha De Danann, the People of the Goddess.

But as the day wore on and drifted into evening and the sun was slipping down in the sky, and there was still no sign of her brothers, she began to despair of ever seeing them again. And for a single moment, her voice broke and she stopped singing . . .

And in the silence she heard the high sweet sound of music. She raised her head and looked around in all directions. At first she could see nothing, but then, on the eastern horizon, she saw two white specks. Fionnuala sang again, and this time she sang with joy and happiness as she watched Aedh and Conn swim slowly towards her.

But of Fiachra, there was no sign.

Both of her brothers had their own stories to tell; of being thrown far and wide, battered and almost drowned, caught and pulled, pushed and twisted by the wind and water until they didn't know where they were. They had met each other by accident as they were following the sound of her voice.

And then the three of them sang together, hoping to call their missing brother to them. But although they sang late into the night, there was no sign of him, and so, one by one, they fell into an exhausted sleep.

That night Fionnuala had a dream. She dreamed that she was back in the hidden blue room in the White Fort where her father had shown her and Aedh their sleeping mother. She saw her mother open her eyes and sit up on her coral bed. The Queen stood up gracefully, her long gown of pale green silk whispering about her as it settled, and then she reached out and took Fionnuala's hand. Together they walked from the smaller room into the larger, circular chamber and, with her small, beautiful hand the Queen pointed to the wall. 'Look,' she whispered.

In the dream Fionnuala could see that the wall was no longer painted blue, and now it showed a picture of a small outcrop of rock with three sleeping swans perched on it. Eva's finger moved and pointed to another part of the wall and there, not too far from the others, was the picture of a small battered and bleeding swan floating on a moonlit sea. The Queen said one more word, 'Fiachra'.

Fionnuala opened her eyes and looked around in confusion, wondering for a moment where she was. She shook her head, trying to clear the images of the dream which had been so real.

And then, as if she heard it coming from a great distance, she remembered her father's words: '. . . she will be watching over you . . . and if you are ever in any great danger . . . she will be there . . .'

Fionnuala immediately awakened her brothers and, although they were unsure whether to believe her or not, they followed her as she set out across the waves. They didn't know where she was going and they could see nothing, but Fionnuala was following the direction she had been shown in her dream. And, just as Aedh was about to say, 'This is a waste of time . . .', they came upon Fiachra, bruised and battered, but alive, just as Fionnuala had seen.

And so the children of Lir were reunited.

Chapter Seven

The three hundred years we spent in the seas of the Strait of Moyle were the hardest of our enchantment. It was a terrible place. We were always cold, wet and hungry, and sometimes it got so cold that the sea froze in a solid sheet all around us and the skin of our feet stuck fast to the icy rock.

'During those times we sang the old songs of our people, for the sounds of our voices would crack the ice and calm the wind. You see, there was a magic in our music, and that magic would often draw the sea creatures to us, and they would bob in the water listening. We saw some strange things too . . .'

The Whale

Conn spotted it first. He tilted his long slender neck from side to side, trying to make out the shape, and then he scrambled up the rock to the highest point and stood looking across the waves.

Fiachra wondered what he was doing. 'What do you see?' he asked.

His twin gave a little shrug of his wings. 'I'm not sure. Come up here and look.'

Fiachra flapped his huge wings and ran up the rock to perch beside his brother. 'What is it?'

Conn pointed with the tip of a wing. 'You tell me,' he said.

Both swans stared out across the waves, looking at a long, broad black and grey shape in the water that seemed to be slowly drifting close to them. It looked like an island, and yet there were no islands even close to their rock. It didn't look dangerous and yet ... these were dangerous waters; you never knew what might happen. Once a huge chunk of ice had been swept up against their rock during the night. The noise had been terrible – a sort of high-pitched screaming sound – but what was even more frightening was that bits and pieces of the ice had scattered all around the rock, and they had been as sharp and as cutting as glass.

Another time a long, many-oared wooden ship with a huge square sail and a monster carved at one end, had come quite close to the rock, and the men on board – big men with yellow hair and plaited beards – had fired arrows at the birds just for fun.

And so the children had learned to be very cautious and careful. Conn took one last look at the thing in the sea, and shook his head. 'I had better get Aedh and Fionnuala.'

Fiachra nodded. 'I'll stay up here and watch.'

While his twin had gone to look for the other two, Fiachra noticed that the strange black object was not just floating aimlessly on the sea – if it had, the sea currents would have been pulled in a different direction. No, this thing was purposefully moving straight for the rock.

He said this to Aedh when he and his sister climbed up to look. His older brother nodded. 'Yes, it is coming over here. I wonder what it is?' he murmured, almost to himself.

'Perhaps it's an island,' Fionnuala said. 'I once heard about islands that float about on the surface of the sea, moving with the waves and currents.'

Aedh looked across the sea again and nodded. 'You could be right. It's certainly big enough to be a small island.'

The strange grey and black object came closer and closer, and now they could see that parts of it were covered with sea-shells and barnacles, and there were long strands of seaweed trailing behind it.

Aedh was just shaking his head, and saying, 'I really don't know what it is,' when the island moved! It came right up out of the water and loomed over the four terrified swans on the tiny rock like a black cliff. Only this cliff had eyes and a huge mouth full of teeth.

It was a whale.

Small black eyes stared down at them, and then the huge mouth opened and the whale spoke – with a voice that was so tiny that it made the children laugh.

'I heard your singing,' the whale squeaked, 'I followed it here.'

Fionnuala bobbed her head. 'I am sorry we laughed then,' she said, 'but we thought you were going to attack us, and then when you spoke . . . well, your voice is . . .' She paused, and looked over at Aedh.

'We were expecting a bigger voice,' her brother said.

'Most people do,' the whale said. 'It's not really fair; here I am, the biggest creature in the world, and I have the smallest voice.'

'It's quite a nice voice though,' Conn said, suddenly feeling sorry for the great creature. 'What's your name?' he asked.

'My name is Jasconius,' he said, 'and I will be famous some day,' he added.

'How do you know?' Aedh asked.

'Because one of the other whales can read the future in the seaweed, and she said that one day I would meet a very great holy man, and I would be remembered for ever.' Jasconius' voice, which had risen higher and higher as he spoke, disappeared into a squeak.

'Can you sing?' Fionnuala asked suddenly.

'I don't know,' Jasconius said. 'I've never tried. But your singing is lovely. I heard it many miles away; some of the other whales heard it also, but we thought that too many of us might frighten you.'

'Sing something,' Fionnuala urged him. 'Your voice is very pure, very lovely . . .'

'What will I sing?'

'Try this,' she said. ' "We sing of a time that is legend,

we speak of a race that is myth, we know of a place of enchantment . . ." '

Jasconius tried to sing the words of the ancient song, but his voice was so thin and high that some of the words were lost. And then Aedh had an idea.

'Whistle it,' he said, 'whistle the tune.'

Jasconius tried it. At first nothing happened, and all that came out were wet, watery spluttering sounds. And then he got it right. His whistle echoed out across the waves, thin and ghostly, hauntingly beautiful. The sea-birds dropped from the sky and landed on his broad back to listen to the lovely sound. Round sleek heads broke the surface of the water as seals popped up to see what was making the noise. Even fish threw themselves wriggling up into the air to see where the sound was coming from.

The whale whistled, and whistled, and whistled, and the sound rolled on and on, changing and changing and changing. The children of Lir sang along with it, and their music was so beautiful that even the choppy waves calmed down. They sang all through the afternoon and on into the night.

At last, when they were all out of breath, they stopped, and one by one, the sea creatures slipped away, the birds took to the skies again, and once again the waves began to lash up on to the rock.

Jasconius the whale bobbed his huge head and his small eyes sparkled with delight. 'Thank you,' he said simply, 'you have given me a great gift.' He backed away from the rock and slowly sank down beneath the waves, but before he disappeared completely, he said, 'I'll teach the other whales.'

Thus the children of Lir taught the whales to sing.

Chapter Eight

'*Everything must come to an end and eventually the second three hundred years passed. We had no way of knowing the time, except that we saw the stars moving through the sky, and we could tell the passing seasons by the length of the day and the height of the sun and moon.*

'*And once again I woke up one morning, and I knew – I just knew – that the second part of our enchantment had passed, and we would now have to move on.*

'*I woke my brothers, and we set off on the final stage of our journey . . .*'

The Holy Man

The four swans flapped their huge wings, making little ripples on the ice water and then slowly, one by one, they rose up into the chill morning air.

The sun had not yet risen and the sky to the east was ablaze with different colours, mostly shades of red and gold, and the low fleecy clouds were touched with pink.

The children of Lir turned to the south and once again they flew over the island of Banba. Almost immediately they began to notice the changes that had taken place over the past three hundred years. Everything looked smaller and where once the great forests had grown, there were now small collections of houses and sometimes even large castles. The long straight lines of roads were everywhere. Along the coasts, the towns were larger and there were many tall-masted ships anchored in the harbours. It made them suddenly realize just how many years they had spent as swans: six hundred years!

On their way over the country they changed direction slightly and flew south, looking for their old home. They flew over Lough Derravaragh where they had spent the first three hundred years and while at the time it had seemed so large, now it, too, looked even smaller, as if it had shrunk over the years. They flew above where the White Fort should have been, but there was nothing there now; the Fort with its shining towers and its roof of beaten gold was gone and in its place was a low grassy mound with bushes and trees growing on it.

And the children of Lir wept there, for they knew that the Age of the Tuatha De Danann was gone, and with it, a lot of the magic had gone out of this world.

They turned away then and headed west for Inish Glora. It was evening before they reached the island and the sun was sinking down into the sea in a magnificent sunset of brilliant reds, golds, pinks and even a touch of blue and green.

Inish Glora was a tiny island off the western coast of Banba. It was uninhabited except for a small colony of seals and hundreds of sea-birds of all shapes and sizes. There wasn't a rock on the island that wasn't touched with white streaks.

The four swans circled the tiny island a few times; after the silence and loneliness of the rock in the Straits of Moyle, they were deafened by the screaming and cawing and chattering of the sea-birds. They at last found a tiny nook under the cliffs and soon fell into an exhausted sleep just as they had done on their last journey three hundred years ago.

They awoke to hear the howling of the wind whipping in off the Western Ocean and the pounding of the waves on the rocky beach. After three hundred years on a stormy sea, they knew the signs: there was a storm brewing.

The storm, which broke around noon, made them wonder if they were doomed to spend another miserable three hundred years cold and wet and hungry. Was there to be no peace for them?

However, the worst of the storm soon passed overhead and rolled in across the mainland. They could hear the thunder booming and the lightning crackling long into the night; it wasn't until the sky in the east was already grey with the dawn that the three boys fell into an uneasy sleep.

Fionnuala waited until she was sure her brothers were asleep before she took to the air and flew the short distance to the mainland. She was looking for some sort of shelter for them all. Summer was almost over and soon the winter storms would come crashing in over the island. She knew that they could not survive another three hundred winters like the last three hundred.

The shoreline along this part of the coast was very rough, with many cliffs and caves and rocky beaches. She soon found what she was looking for: a large dry cave, with a small opening big enough to allow the swans in, but not so big that it could not be blocked up from inside with stones to keep out the wind and rain. It was perfect.

When she returned to the island, she found her brothers awake and worried. They had been about to set out in search of her, thinking that perhaps she had been washed off the island by a wave.

'We didn't know what had happened,' Aedh said.

'I'm sorry,' she said. 'I thought I would be back before you had woken up.'

'But where were you?' Conn asked.

Fionnuala pointed with one long-feathered wing towards the mainland. 'I was over there looking for a better place for us to spend the next three hundred years.'

'But I thought we had to spend all our time here on Inish Glora,' Fiachra said.

The tall swan shook her small head gracefully. 'When

our stepmother cursed us, she said that we must spend our time in the waters about Inish Glora.' She pointed towards the mainland again. 'And those waters are about Inish Glora.'

'So there is nothing stopping us from settling there?' Conn asked.

Fionnuala shook her head. 'Nothing.'

And so they settled on the mainland in the cave that Fionnuala had found, and they spent the first few weeks there, warm and dry for the first time for so long.

Then one morning Conn and Fiachra, who had gone flying in over the mainland, returned very excited. The two large birds swooped down low over the beach, extended their huge wings and settled down in a shower of sand. Aedh and Fionnuala came running, thinking something was wrong.

'You must come,' Conn said breathlessly, before they could say anything.

'Yes, it's perfect, just perfect,' his twin said. 'You must come.'

So, a little puzzled and amused, Aedh and Fionnuala followed their younger brothers as they flew above the cliffs and a short distance inland. The twins swung around to the south and then dipped down, and there below them was a beautiful sheltered lake. It was a saltwater lake, and was connected to the sea by a rushing underground river; and so it didn't break their *geasa*, the special spell their stepmother had cast over them, since it was the same water that washed over Inish Glora. The lake was surrounded on three sides by trees and bushes and on the fourth by a small green field.

It was indeed perfect, and so they settled there.

In the evenings, as the sun was setting in the Western

Ocean, they would sing together, and then the birds of the air and the birds of the sea would gather on the branches of the trees, in the bushes and on the water, and listen spellbound to the four beautifully blended voices. In time that small lake became known as the Lake of Birds.

Time passed slowly for the four children of Lir and to measure the passing days, each morning they would take one small round stone from the beach and place it by the side of the lake. Now, when this pile had grown quite large, an old man came and settled down by the side of their lake.

He was small and frail-looking, with long grey hair and an equally long grey beard, and he moved slowly and carefully, leaning on a tall stick. He wore a short robe that had once been white, but which was now a dirty grey. It was tied about the middle by a piece of rough cord.

The first thing the old man did when he came to the lake was to start building a small round hut in the small field at the eastern end of the lake. Early every morning he would go down to the beach and, with a thick piece of rope, he would drag the stones up along the sands, up the steep path and across the field to the side of the lake. He placed the stones one on top of the other and used wet clay to cement them together.

Sometimes the larger blocks were too heavy for the old man and he would fall into an exhausted sleep on the ground beside them, after only moving them a little way.

But when he awoke he would find the stones in place.

What the old man didn't know was that while he slept, the four swans would each take one end of the rope and, by using their powerful wings, lift the stone into place.

The children watched the old man curiously. He was the first human they had seen in a long time, and Fionnuala said that he reminded her of the druids, the holy men who had been around when she was a child.

Conn then wanted to know what sort of holy man he was, because the druids usually wore long white robes and carried little golden sickles and sometimes wore crowns of holly and oak. 'I've never seen any druid like him,' he finished.

Fionnuala didn't answer for a while, and then she said, very quietly, and with such a strange note in her voice that her brothers looked at her. 'Do you remember when our stepmother put her curse on us, she said that we would not be released until the bell of the New God was heard in the land?'

Aedh nodded, and then he looked across at the old man. 'If he is a holy man,' he said, 'do you think he is a follower of this new god?'

'I don't know,' Fionnuala said, 'should we ask him?'

One by one the children nodded. The four swans drifted across the waters of the lake towards the old man, who was plastering his little hut with a thick covering of mud. He was singing quietly to himself in a strange, harsh-sounding language. They waited in the water until he had finished and then he came down and knelt in the shallow water to wash the mud and clay off his hands. He smiled at the four swans.

'Well, how are you today? I haven't seen you four for a long time. I'm afraid I've no bread for you, but I will be making some tomorrow, and I'll make sure I keep some for you then.' When the old man made bread – short flat loaves and little buns – he usually threw some into the water for the birds.

'That would be very nice, thank you,' Fionnuala said quietly.

The old man screamed and jumped backwards with fright, landing with a splash in the water. He sat there looking at the swans in amazement.

Had one of them just spoken to him?

'I'm sorry if I frightened you,' Fionnuala said drifting closer.

The old man scrambled backwards out of the water and then he moved his right hand up and across in a strange gesture and spoke in the same foreign language in which he had been singing. He then stood up as if he were waiting for something to happen – almost as if he expected the four swans to disappear in a puff of smoke.

'Oh,' he said at last, when nothing happened, 'you are real.'

'Of course,' Aedh said, coming right into the water's edge, 'what did you expect?'

'You can both talk,' he said in astonishment.

'We all talk,' the swan with the girl's voice said. 'My name is Fionnuala, and these are my brothers, Aedh, Conn and Fiachra.'

'Talking swans,' the old man said to himself, and then his sharp eyes lit up with delight and understanding. 'Of course, the children of Lir!'

'You know about us?' Aedh asked in amazement.

'But of course; all Erin knows the legend of the Children of Lir.'

'A legend?' Conn asked.

The old man nodded. 'Aye, a legend; you and all the rest of your magical race have long since passed into legend.' He shook his head sadly, and then, suddenly remembering, he said, 'My name is Mochaomhog, but most people call me Mocha.'

'Are you a holy man?' Fiachra asked.

Mocha nodded. 'I am a follower of Our Lord Jesus Christ,' he said and made the same crossing sign in the air.

'Tell us about this Christ,' Fionnuala said. 'When our stepmother enchanted us, she said that we would not be released until the bell of the New God was heard in our land.'

And so Mocha sat down by the side of the lake and spoke to the children of Lir about the birth and life of Jesus, and he spoke of the followers of Christ and of Patrick, who had carried the Word to Erin, and whose follower Mocha was.

Chapter Nine

'My story is nearly done now; only a little remains to be told, and I will tell it quickly.

'We stayed with Mocha the Holy for many years. He read to us from his holy books and we listened to the Word of God and in return we sang in the tiny church he had built. Soon people came from miles around just to listen to us. They said that we had the voices of angels.

'At that time Mocha was collecting pieces of metal. The people brought him old swords and shields, arrow-heads and the rusted tops of spears, which he gave to the local blacksmith to make into a bell.

'We were very excited because the moment Mocha rang that bell for the first time, we would change back into our human forms.

'But on the day the bell was to be hung, a terrible thing happened.

'We had all gathered in the small church early one morning. Mocha was about to bless the beautifully carved bell before ringing it, when suddenly there was a rattling of metal, shouts and the sound of horses' hooves outside . . .'

The End of Enchantment

A tall shadow darkened the doorway. Mocha looked up from the altar and then opened his mouth in surprise as a warrior dressed in armour and a long flowing cloak stepped into the tiny round church. He had a sword in his hand, and he was wearing a horned helmet.

'What do you want?' Mocha demanded.

The warrior pointed with his sword at the four swans sitting to one side of the small stone altar. 'Them,' he said simply.

'No!' the old priest shouted, and then he added in a quieter voice, 'How dare you come into the House of God with a sword in your hand and without removing your helmet?'

The warrior took one step forward and lifted up his sword, which reflected the light from the candles, turning it into a shining bar of gold. 'I am Lairgren,' he said coldly. 'I am the King of Connaught, and I have promised these singing swans to my wife Dessa, the Princess of Munster.'

'You cannot have them,' Mocha said, and stood in front of the swans.

'If you try to stop me, old man,' the King said loudly, 'I will have my men pull your church down and throw the stones into the lake.'

'You wouldn't dare ...' Mocha began. The King smiled, showing his teeth. 'I would.'

Fionnuala flapped her wings, gently pushing the old man aside. 'We won't allow you to do this for us. You have worked long and hard, and we won't see your church destroyed.'

Lairgren was startled when he heard the swan speaking with a young girl's voice; it was true then. Up to now he had thought it was only another fairy story. But the woman he had married had a terrible temper and she was very greedy also, and when he had foolishly told her that he would give her anything she wanted for a wedding present, she had demanded the singing swans.

The king called in four of his men and each took one of the birds and carried it outside where a chariot with a cage was waiting.

But they had barely stepped outside the church when a bell began to toll, its high sweet notes ringing across the waters of the lake and echoing off the stones. For a single moment everything seemed to stop, and then the four men carrying the swans dropped their bundles with shouts of horror. A sudden breeze had sprung up and blown across the waters of the lake, gathering up the mist that still clung to it into a solid ball, sweeping in over the land and covering the four swans. The ball of grey-white mist grew and grew. Tiny bubbles of all the colours of the rainbow gathered and burst on its surface. The four swans now were completely hidden behind a solid wall of mist which quickly changed from green to blue to yellow and then back to blue again. There was a strange smell in the air, like the smell of fish, salt and seaweed when the tide goes out.

And then the magical breeze blew again and slowly, slowly, slowly the mist began to disperse in a light blue cloud.

The swans were gone.

And in their place stood four small figures; three pale-skinned men and one delicately beautiful woman. The woman stepped forward and smiled. 'We are the children of Lir,' she said, her voice as sweet as a song.

'And so we changed back into our human forms. When Lairgren saw us, he grew frightened and rode away with his men, and we never saw him again. We were baptized that same day by Mocha, and we became followers of Christ.

'That was many years ago now. Mocha is gone and the world is changing quickly. It is even stranger now than it was when we had finished our nine hundred years as swans.

'Once I thought we were doomed to spend the rest of our long, long lives here in this world, but I had forgotten that even the Tuatha De Danann do not Sleep for ever . . .

'My brothers are waiting for me, I must go now. I don't know where, but our mother came for us this morning. We are going home.'

The song is sung,
The tale is told,
The children returned,
and gone,
But their magic lingers on.